Milly and Molly

For my grandchildren
Thomas, Harry, Ella and Madeleine

Part of the proceeds from the sale of this book goes to The Friends of Milly, Molly Inc.,
a charity, which aims to promote the acceptance of diversity and the learning of life
skills through literacy - *'for every child, a book.'*

Milly, Molly and the Stowaways

Copyright © MM House Publishing, 2003

Gill Pittar and Cris Morrell assert the moral right to
be recognised as the author and illustrator of this work.

Published by
MM House Publishing
P O Box 539
Gisborne, New Zealand
email: books@millymolly.com

Printed by Rhythm Consolidated Berhad, Malaysia

ISBN: 1-86972-026-1

10   9   8   7   6   5   4   3   2   1

Milly, Molly
and the
Stowaways

"We may look different
but we feel the same."

The stage was set.
The audience was seated.

2

"This play's going to be scary."

"It's about stowaways."

"And walking the plank."

"It's about drowning."

"And being eaten by sharks."

The boys all had their say.

"We don't want to watch," said Milly and Molly.
Miss Blythe stood up. "Quiet please," she
said firmly.

The boys fidgeted.
The girls whispered.

Then the curtain went up and there was silence. The Captain sat at his desk.

"Bring in the stowaways, one by one,"
he ordered the First Mate.
"Let's see what they can do for their keep."

8

The first stowaway pulled a harmonica
from his pocket and played a beautiful tune.
The Captain clapped. "You can play for
your keep."

The second stowaway lifted her head
and sang a beautiful song.
The Captain clapped. "You can sing for
your keep."

The third stowaway pulled out a pad and
pencil and sketched a beautiful boat.
The Captain clapped. "You can sketch for
your keep."

The fourth stowaway folded her arms behind
her back and performed a beautiful jig.
The Captain clapped. "You can dance for
your keep."

The fifth stowaway held a notebook
and opened his mouth but he couldn't
make a sound.

He twisted and strained, clutching the
notebook, but he still couldn't make a sound.

The audience held their breath. Milly and
Molly disappeared under their seats.

The Captain shook his head.
The first stowaway stepped up. "Please
...wait. I can help." He took the notebook
and read a beautiful poem.

The Captain clapped. "You!" he said to the
fifth stowaway. "You can write poetry for
your keep."

"But tell me one thing," said the Captain.
"Why are you stowing away on my ship
when you all have such beautiful talents?"

"We thought we could prove our worth before being returned to shore," said the first stowaway. "You see, no one gives us a chance." "I don't understand," said the Captain.

"I have a brain injury," said the first
stowaway with the harmonica.
"I'm blind," said the second stowaway with
the beautiful voice.
"I'm deaf," said the third stowaway with
the sketchpad.

"I have no hands," said the fourth
stowaway with the dancing legs.
"I st-st-stutter," said the fifth stowaway
with the notebook of poems.

The Captain clapped and clapped.
"Now I understand," he said. "How about
we see the world?"
"Full steam ahead!" he cried.

The First Mate cheered. The stowaways
jumped for joy.

The cast lined up to take a bow. The audience
rose to their feet and clapped and cheered.
"We want to be stowaways too," they shouted.

Milly, Molly and the Stowaways

The value implicitly expressed in this story is 'sense of worth' – feeling of value; - feeling needed and useful.

The captain didn't judge the stowaways by their handicaps. Instead, he valued and rewarded each stowaway for his or her sense of worth.

"We may look different but we feel the same."

B O O K S

Other picture books in the Milly, Molly series include:

- Milly, Molly and Jimmy's Seeds   ISBN 1-86972-000-8
- Milly, Molly and Beefy   ISBN 1-86972-006-7
- Milly, Molly and Pet Day   ISBN 1-86972-004-0
- Milly, Molly and Oink   ISBN 1-86972-002-4
- Milly and Molly Go Camping   ISBN 1-86972-003-2
- Milly, Molly and Betelgeuse   ISBN 1-86972-005-9
- Milly, Molly and Taffy Bogle   ISBN 1-86972-001-6
- Milly, Molly and Alf   ISBN 1-86972-018-0
- Milly, Molly and Sock Heaven   ISBN 1-86972-015-6
- Milly, Molly and the Sunhat   ISBN 1-86972-016-4
- Milly, Molly and Special Friends   ISBN 1-86972-017-2
- Milly, Molly and Different Dads   ISBN 1-86972-019-9
- Milly, Molly and Aunt Maude   ISBN 1-86972-014-8
- Milly, Molly and Grandpa Friday   ISBN 1-86972-029-6
- Milly, Molly and Henry   ISBN 1-86972-030-X
- Milly, Molly and the Secret Scarves   ISBN 1-86972-027-X
- Milly, Molly and the Tree Hut   ISBN 1-86972-028-8
- Milly, Molly and What Was That   ISBN 1-86972-031-8